THE MISUNDERSTOOD LIFE of Brutus

By: Sandy Register

Illustrated By: Arianna Grinager

iUniverse books may be ordered through booksellers or by contacting:

iUniverse
1663 Liberty Drive
Bloomington, IN 47403
www.iuniverse.com
844-349-9409

Because of the dynamic nature of the Internet, any web addresses or links contained in this book may have changed since publication and may no longer be valid. The views expressed in this work are solely those of the author and do not necessarily reflect the views of the publisher, and the publisher hereby disclaims any responsibility for them.

Any people depicted in stock imagery provided by Getty Images are models, and such images are being used for illustrative purposes only.
Certain stock imagery © Getty Images.

ISBN: 978-1-6632-2073-8 (sc)
ISBN: 978-1-6632-2074-5 (e)

Library of Congress Control Number: 2021911977

Print information available on the last page.

iUniverse rev. date: 07/15/2021

This book is dedicated to:

In loving memory
Marc Anthony Garcia
June 29, 1984 to December 20, 2014

Without him Brutus' story would not be possible.

My name is Brutus. Brutus Garcia. I am almost 4 years old and like any one who is almost 4 years old my life is misunderstood. There are many things that confuse me and I just don't understand. I have a lot to learn.

Did I mention that I am a dog? Well I am. I am a Boston terrier mix. I am brown, brindle, and white. I am adorable. Everyone says so. The first thing that I am misunderstood about is my name .Don't get me wrong, I love my name. I know a lot of thought went into choosing it for me

Here is the problem with my name. Doesn't the name Brutus sound like I should be a mean and tough dog? But I'm not at all. I am a lover not a fighter. I don't even know how to fight!

When people hear my name they expect to see a mean and tough dog. A dog that can protect his family from danger. But since I am only almost 4 years old I don't have enough life experiences to even know what danger is.

So I just bark and carry on like I think a mean dog would. I hope that I will just scare away anyone I think might be a danger. I guess it works because they just keep on going.

When I see someone riding a bicycle, pushing a baby stroller, riding a skate board, or just a group of big kids walking down the street, I don't know what they are up to. It seems to me that they are up to no good. There is cause for alarm.

"NEVER UNDERESTIMATE THE ACTIONS OF THOSE DOING THINGS YOU DON'T UNDERSTAND". Good advice. Don't forget it. It's just as important as staying away from electricity and strangers.

I think if I was named something sissy like Beau Beau, Muffin, Mikey, Toby, or Nancy, I would handle these dangerous situations differently. I would probably just run in the house with my tail between my legs and hide. Not protecting my family at all, So I am glad that my name is Brutus and I protect my family from danger Aren't you glad too?

I don't know how other dogs have it, but I have it pretty good. The lady I live with and call "MOM", Isn't my dog mom. She is a lady. And a nice lady at that. Her name is Kiley. She is very nice. She loves me and I love her.

I love her to the moon and back. I heard someone say that the other day and I thought it sounded cool. So I stole it. I am a copy cat. Which is one of the things I am misunderstood about, why is it called a copy cat instead of a copy dog? No one knows, that is just the way it is. See what I mean?

I came to live with Kiley when I was very young and very small. I was adorable. I still am. I couldn't ask for a better life. If they would have named me "Lucky" it would fit. I am lucky. I have never been mistreated, I am only misunderstood.

My life could have turned out a lot different. Everyone has a story. Let me tell you mine.

My dog mom was homeless. In the dog world she was called a stray. She was found wandering the streets. She was tired, dirty, hungry and worried. She was about to have puppies. She didn't have a home for us. She was found by a nice man who took her in and took very good care of her. After she had her puppies he took good care of us too.

The dog catcher man could have got her and taken her in to the dog pound which is a dog jail. We could have been born in jail! We would have been treated like criminals but we had done nothing wrong. I could have been named something like "Mad Dog", "Butch", "Lifer" or "Otis". That would be so scary. I have heard stories about that pound place and it doesn't sound like anywhere I would want to be. Ever.

The other day I had quite a scare. I heard some people talking about something being wrong with my pa. I thought my dad had been found and something was wrong with him. But then I thought "wait just a dog gone minute", If I have never met my pa then how do they know anything about him? Well come to find out there was something wrong with my foot and in the dog world this is called my paw! So they weren't talking about my dad at all. See what I mean about having a lot to learn?

Because my paw was painful I had to go this place called a Betternarian clinic. This is a place where they can make sick or injured animals better. I didn't like it there at all. They didn't like me either. So I did what I always do when I think there is danger. I barked and growled and carried on like I thought I should.

And do you know what they did? The wrote in big letters on my medical chart "MEAN DOG-BEWARE" That was so they would be warned that there was a mean dog in the office every time I went there. That wasn't very nice. I was just in a lot of pain and I was scared. Kiley didn't think it was very nice either. So we never had to go there again. See I told you she was nice.

So we found a new Betternarian Clinic to go to. The doctor there loves me a lot. I don't quite know what to think of her. She loves me so much that she fixes things that aren't broken. I had to get dropped off there one morning to get fixed. I can't for the life of me even tell you what was broken. But I am fixed now.

I won a special place in Kileys heart because I was a birthday present. Oh I just had a shuddering thought. I could have been named "Happy". Yikes, don't you agree?

People like Kiley have it kind of hard. They have responsibilities. It takes a lot of patience and responsibilities to raise a dog like me. People go to a place they call work. No matter what they do at work everyone calls it work. They go there a lot. I got to go to Kileys work one day. I got to tell you I wasn't impressed. I had to just sit and behave myself. In a room full of strangers!

STRANGER DANGER. I'm on it. Not a good idea. I started barking and growling at Kiley's work friends and her boss. I never had to go there again.

Sometimes Kiley has to go on business trips. I don't understand it. When I have business to do, I just go out in the yard and do my business and I'm done with it. When Kiley goes on a business trip she has to pack a suitcase, buy an airline ticket, and fly off to places called Houston, Nashville, Seattle, DC or Vegas.

When Kiley goes on business trips she is gone a long time. About 3 days! I am still too young to stay by myself. So my grandma comes to take care of me. A grandma is like a mom only she is older, nicer, and smarter than a mom. She calls me her GRANDDOG, but there is nothing GRAND about me. I am just a medium size dog. But she thinks I am a GRAND dog and that is why I love her so much. But don't you think if I were a GRAND dog I would be called something like William, Harry, Royal, King or Archie?

Well, whether you are a dog, a cat, or a person life can be full of things that we just don't understand. We all have questions that we don't have the answers to. That's okay. We will figure it all out. But there is one thing I don't think I will ever understand and I am glad that I don't have to. Cats!

About cats. Don't you think that they get confused about a litter of kitties and kitty litter? That's deep. I am glad I am not a cat. I'm not even a cat person; in fact I don't even like cats. I think they are silly. No matter how many lives they have.

Well my friends a business trip awaits me and I got to go. I'm sure there will be many more things that we don't understand and we will try to figure things out later. But remember I love you to the moon and back.

THE END

Printed in the United States
by Baker & Taylor Publisher Services